An
Elegy for
Easterly

Faber
Sto

Petina Gappah is an international lawyer and writer who was born in Kitwe, Zambia and raised in Zimbabwe. She is the author of *An Elegy for Easterly*, *The Book of Memory* and *Rotten Row*. Her work has been shortlisted for, among others, the Orwell Prize, the *Sunday Times* EFG Short Story Award, the *Los Angeles Times* Book Award, the PEN America Open Book Award and the Prix Femina (Étrangers). She is the 2009 recipient of the *Guardian* First Book Award and the 2016 recipient of the McKitterick Prize from the Society of Authors.

Petina Gappah

An Elegy for Easterly

Faber Stories

ff

First published in this single edition in 2019
by Faber & Faber Limited
Bloomsbury House
74–77 Great Russell Street
London WC1B 3DA
First published in *An Elegy for Easterly* in 2009

Typeset by Faber & Faber Limited
Printed and bound by CPI Group (UK) Ltd, Croydon, CR0 4YY

The right of Petina Gappah to be identified as author of this work
has been asserted in accordance with Section 77 of the Copyright,
Designs and Patents Act 1988

A CIP record for this book
is available from the British Library

ISBN 978–0–571–35179–4

MIX
Paper from
responsible sources
FSC® C020471
FSC
www.fsc.org

10 9 8 7 6 5 4 3 2 1

It was the children who first noticed that there was something different about the woman they called Martha Mupengo. They followed her, as they often did, past the houses in Easterly Farm, houses of pole and mud, of thick black plastic sheeting for walls and clear plastic for windows, houses that erupted without City permission, unnumbered houses identified only by reference to the names of their occupants. They followed her past *Mai*James's house, *Mai* Toby's house, past the house occupied by Josephat's wife, and her husband Josephat when he was on leave from the mine, past the house of the newly arrived couple that no one really knew, all the way past the people waiting with plastic buckets to take water from Easterly's only tap.

'Where are you going, Martha Mupengo?' they sang.

1

She turned and showed them her teeth.

'May I have twenty cents,' she said, and lifted up her dress.

Giddy with delight, the children pointed at her nakedness. '*Hee, haana bhurugwa*,' they screeched. '*Hee*, Martha has no panties on, she has no panties on.'

However many times Martha Mupengo lifted her dress, they did not tire of it. As the dress fell back, it occurred to the children that there was something a little different, a little slow about her. It took a few seconds for Tobias, the sharp-eyed leader of Easterly's Under-Eights, to notice that the something different was the protrusion of the stomach above the thatch of dark hair.

'*Haa*, Martha Mupengo is swollen,' he shouted. 'What have you eaten, Martha Mupengo?'

The children took up the chorus. 'What have you eaten, Martha Mupengo?' they shouted as they followed her to her house in the far corner of Easterly. Superstition prevented them from entering. Tobias's chief rival Tawanda, a boy with four missing teeth and eyes as big as Tobias's ears were wide, threw a stick through the open doorway. Not to be outdone, Tobias picked up an empty baked beans can. He struck a metal rod against it, but even this clanging did not bring Martha out. After a few more failed stratagems, they moved on.

Their mouths and lungs took in the smoke-soaked smell of Easterly: smoke from outside cooking, smoke wafting in through the trees from the roadside where women roasted maize in the rainy season, smoke from burning grass three fields away, cigarette smoke.

They kicked the empty can to each other until hunger and a sudden quarrel propelled Tobias to his family's house.

His mother *Mai*Toby sat at her sewing machine. Around her were the swirls of fabric, sky-blue, magnolia, buttermilk and bolts of white stuffing for the duvets that she made to sell. The small generator powering the sewing machine sent diesel fumes into the room. Tobias raised his voice above the machine.

'I am hungry.'

'I have not yet cooked, go and play.'

He sat in the doorway. He remembered Martha.

'Martha's stomach is swollen,' he said.

'Mmmm?'

'Martha, she is ever so swollen.'

'Ho nhai?'

4

He indicated with his arms and said again, 'Her stomach is this big.'

'Hoo,' his mother said without looking up. One half of her mind was on the work before her, and the other half was on another matter: should she put elaborate candlewick on this duvet, or should she walk all the way to *Mai*-James's to make a call to follow up on that ten million she was owed? *Mai*James operated a phone shop from her house. She walked her customers to a hillock at the end of the Farm and stood next to them as they telephoned. On the hillock, *Mai*James opened the two mobiles she had, and inserted one SIM card after the other to see which would get the best reception. Her phone was convenient, but there was this: from *Mai*James came most of the gossip at Easterly.

———

In her home, Martha slept.

Her name and memory, past and dreams, were lost in the foggy corners of her mind. She lived in the house and slept on the mattress on which a man called Titus Zunguza had killed first his woman, and then himself. The cries of Titus Zunguza's woman were loud in the night. Help would have come, for the people of Easterly lived to avoid the police. But by the time Godwills Mabhena who lived next to *Mai*James had crossed the distance to Titus Zunguza's house, by the time he had roused a sufficient number of neighbours to enter, help had come too late. And when the police did come, they were satisfied that it was no more than what it was.

Six months after the deaths, when blood still showed on the mattress, Martha claimed the house simply by moving in. As the lone place of horror on Easterly, the house was left untouched; even the children acted out the terror of the murderous night from a distance.

They called her Martha because *Mai*James said that was exactly how her husband's niece Martha had looked in the last days when her illness had spread to her brain. 'That is how she looked,' *Mai*James said. 'Just like that, nothing in the face, just a smile, and nothing more.'

It was the children who called her Mupengo, Mudunyaz, and other variations on lunacy. The name Martha Mupengo stuck more than the others, becoming as much a part of her as the dresses of flamboyantly coloured material, bright with exotic flowers, poppies and roses and bluebells, dresses that had belonged to Titus Zunguza's woman and that hung on Martha's thin frame.

7

She was not one of the early arrivals to Easterly.

She did not come with those who arrived after the government cleaned the townships to make Harare pristine for the three-day visit of the Queen of England. All the women who walk alone at night are prostitutes, the government said – lock them up, the Queen is coming. There are illegal structures in the townships they said – clean them up. The townships are too full of people, they said, gather them up and put them in the places the Queen will not see, in Porta Farm, in Hatcliffe, in Dzivaresekwa Extension, in Easterly. Allow them temporary structures, and promise them real walls and doors, windows and toilets.

And so the government hid away the poverty, the people put on plastic smiles and the City Council planted new flowers in the streets.

Long after the memories of the Queen's visit had faded, and the broken arms of the arrested women were healed, Easterly Farm took root. The first wave was followed by a second, and by another, and yet another. Martha did not come with the first wave, nor with the next, nor with the one after that. She just appeared, as though from nowhere.

She did not speak beyond her request for twenty cents.

Tobias, Tawanda and the children thought this just another sign of madness, she was asking for something that you could not give. Senses, they thought, we have five senses and not twenty, until Tobias's father, *Ba*Toby, the only adult who took the trouble to explain anything, told them that cents were an old type of money, coins of different colours. In the days before a loaf of bread cost half a million dollars, he said, one hundred cents made one dollar. He took down an old tin and said as he opened it, 'We used the coins as recently as 2000.'

'Eight years ago, I remember,' said an older child. 'The five cent coin had a rabbit, the ten cents a baobab tree. The twenty had . . . had . . . umm, *I* know . . . Beit Bridge.'

'Birchenough Bridge,' said *Ba*Toby. 'Beitbridge is one word, and it is a town.'

'The fifty had the setting sun . . .'

'Rising sun,' said *Ba*Toby.

'And the dollar coin had the Zimbabwe Ruins,' the child continued.

'Well done, good effort,' said *Ba*Toby. He spoke in the hearty tones of Mr Barwa, his history teacher from Form Three. He, too, would have liked to teach the wonders of Uthman dan Fodio's Caliphate of Sokoto and Tshaka's horseshoe battle formation, but providence in the shape of the premature arrival of Tobias had deposited him, grease under his nails, at the corner of Kaguvi Street and High Road, where he repaired broken-down cars for a living.

As he showed them the coins, he remembered a joke he had heard that day. He repeated it to the children. 'Before the President was elected, the Zimbabwe Ruins were a prehistoric monument in Masvingo province. Now, the Zimbabwe Ruins extend to the whole country.' The children looked at him blankly, before running off to play, leaving him to laugh with his whole body shaking.

The children understood that Martha's memory was frozen in the time before they

11

could remember, the time of once upon a time, of good times that their parents had known, of days when it was normal to have more than leftovers for breakfast. 'We danced to records at Christmas,' *Ba*Toby was heard to say. 'We had reason to dance then, we had our Christmas bonuses.'

Like Martha's madness, the Christmas records and bonuses were added to the games of Easterly Farm, and for the children it was Christmas at least once a week.

In the mornings, the men and women of Easterly washed off their sleep smells in buckets of water that had to be heated in the winter. They dressed in shirts and skirts ironed straight with coal irons. In their smart clothes, thumbing lifts at the side of the road, they looked like anyone else, from anywhere else.

The formal workers of Easterly Farm were a small number: the country had become a nation of informal traders. They were blessed to have four countries bordering them: to the north, Zambia, formerly one-Zambia-one-nation-one-robot-one-petrol-station, Zambia of the joke currency had become the stop of choice for scarce commodities; to the east, Mozambique, their almost colony, *kudanana kwevanhu veMozambiki neZimbabwe*, reliant on their solidarity pacts and friendship treaties, on their soldiers guarding the Beira Corridor; this Mozambique was now the place to withdraw the foreign money not available in their own country; to the west, Botswana, how they had laughed at Botswana with no building taller than thirteen storeys, the same Botswana that now said it was so full of them that it was erecting a fence along the border to electrify their dreams of three meals a day; and, to the south, cupping Africa in her hands of plenty, Ndazo, *ku*South, Joni, Jubheki, Wenera, South Africa.

They had become a nation of traders.

So it was that in the mornings, the women of the markets rose early and caught the mouth of the rooster. In Mbare Musika they loaded boxes of leaf vegetables, tomatoes and onions, sacks of potatoes, yellow bursts of spotted bananas. They took omnibuses to Mufakose, to Kuwadzana and Glen Norah to stand in stalls and coax customers.

'One million for two, five million for six, only half a million.'

'Nice bananas, nice tomatoes, buy some nice bananas.'

They sang out their wares as they walked the streets.

'*M*bambaira, muriwo, *ma*tomato, onion, *ma*banana, *ma*orange.'

The men and boys went to Siyaso, the smoke-laced second-hand market where the expectation of profit defied the experience of breaking even. In this section, hubcaps, bolts, nuts, adaptors, spanners. Over there, an entire floor given over to the mysterious bits, spiked and heavy, rusted and box-shaped, that give life to appliances. In the next, sink separators, plugs, cellphone chargers. Under the bridge, cobblers making *manyatera* sandals out of disused tyres. The shoes were made to measure, 'Just put your foot here, *blaz*,' the sole of the shoe sketched out and cut out around the foot, a hammering of strips of old tyre onto the sole, and

15

lo, fifteen-minute footwear. In Siyaso, it was not unknown for a man whose car had been relieved of its radio or hubcaps to buy them back from the man into whose hands they had fallen. At a discount.

On the other side of Mbare, among the *zhing-zhong* products from China, the shiny clothes spelling out cheerful poverty, the glittery tank tops and body tops imported in striped carrier bags from Dubai, among the Gucchii bags and Prader shoes, among the Louise Vilton bags, the boys of Mupedzanhamo competed to get the best customers.

'Sister, you look so smart. With this on you, you will be smarter still.'

'Leave my sister be, she was looking this way, this way, sister.'

'Sister, sister, this way.'

'This way, sister.'

'This way.'

'Sister.'

'My *si.*'

They spent the day away from Easterly Farm, in the city, in the markets, in Siyaso. They stood at street corners selling belts with steel buckles, brightly coloured Afro combs studded with mirrors, individual cigarettes smoked over a newspaper read at a street corner, boiled eggs with pinches of salt in brown paper. They passed on whispered rumours about the President's health.

'He tumbled off the stairs of a plane in Malaysia.'

'Yah, that is what happens to people who suffer from foot and mouth, people who talk too much and travel too much.'

At the end of the day, smelling of heat and dust, they packed up their wares and they returned to Easterly Farm, to be greeted again by Martha Mupengo.

'May I have twenty cents,' she said, and lifted up her dress.

Josephat's wife was the first of the adults to recognise Martha's condition. She and Josephat, when he was home from the mine, lived in the house that had belonged to her aunt. It was five years since Josephat's wife had married Josephat. She had tasted the sound of her new identity on her tongue and liked it so much that she called herself nothing else. 'This is Josephat's wife,' she said when she spoke into the telephone on the hillock above the Farm. 'Hello, hello. It's Josephat's wife. Josephat's *wife*.'

'It is like she is the first woman in the

entire world to be married,' *Mai*James said to *Mai*Toby.

'*Vatsva vetsambo*,' said *Mai*Toby. 'Give her another couple of years of marriage and she will be smiling on the other side of her face.'

On that day, Josephat's wife was walking slowly back into Easterly, careful not to dislodge the thick wad of cotton the nurses had placed between her legs. Like air seeping out of the wheels of a bus on the rocky road to Magunje, the joy was seeping out of the marriage. *Kusvodza*, they called it at the hospital, which put her in mind of *kusvedza*, slipping, sliding, and that is what was happening, the babies slipped and slid out in a mess of blood and flesh. She had moved to Easterly Farm to protect the unborn, fleeing from Mutoko where Josephat had brought her as a bride. After three miscarriages, she believed the tales of witchcraft that were whispered about Josephat's aunts on his father's side.

'They are eating my children,' she declared, when Josephat found her at his two-roomed house at Hartley Mine near Chegutu. She stayed only six months. After another miscarriage, she remembered the whispers about the foreman's wife, and her friend Rebecca who kept the bottle store.

'They are eating my children,' she said and moved to her aunt's house in Mbare. There she remained until the family was evicted and set up home in Easterly Farm. After another miscarriage, she said to her aunt, 'You are eating my children.'

Her aunt did not take this well. She had, after all, sympathised with Josephat's wife, even telling her of other people who might be eating her children. In the fight that followed, Josephat's wife lost a tooth and all the buttons of her dress. Then the younger brother of the aunt's husband had died. By throwing the dead brother's widow and her young family out of their house in Chitungwiza, the aunt and her husband acquired a new house, and Josephat's wife was left in Easterly.

In the evenings, she read from her Bible, her lips moving as she read the promises for the faithful. 'Is there any among you that is sick? Let him call for the elders of the Church; and let them pray over him, anointing him with oil in the name of the Lord. And the prayer of faith shall save the sick.'

From church to church she flitted, worshipping in township backrooms while drunken revellers roared outside, mosquitoes gorging on her blood in the open fields as she prayed among the white-clad, visiting prophets with shaven heads and hooked staffs who put their hands on her head and on her breasts. At the Sacred Church of the Anointed Lamb, at the Temple of God's Deliverance, at the Church of Our Saviour of Glad Tidings, she cried out her need in the language of tongues. She chased a child as her fellow penitents chased salvation, chased a path out of penury, chased away the unbearable heaviness of loneliness, sought some kind of redemption. And if the Lord remained deaf, that was because she had not asked hard enough, prayed hard enough, she thought.

She was walking past *Mai*Toby's house on the way to her own, when she remembered that *Mai*Toby had told her about a new church whose congregation prayed in the field near Sherwood Golf Course in Sentosa. 'You can't miss them,' *Mai*Toby had said. 'You go along Quendon, until you reach the Tokwe flats. They worship under a tree on which hangs a big square flag; it has a white cross on a red background.'

It means taking three commuter omnibuses, Josephat's wife thought. First, the omnibus to Mabvuku, then one to town. She would have to walk for fifteen or so minutes from Fourth Street to Leopold Takawira, take an omnibus to Avondale and walk for another forty-five minutes to Sentosa.

I will rise at five, she thought, and catch the mouth of the rooster.

She remembered that she had not been able to reach her husband at the mine to tell him of yet another miscarriage. That thought directed her feet towards *Mai*James's house. It was then that she saw Martha. The woman

23

did not need to lift her dress to reveal the full contours of pregnancy. The sight reached that part of Josephat's wife's spirit that still remained to be crushed. She ran past Martha, they brushed shoulders, Martha staggered a little, but Josephat's wife moved on.

'May I have twenty cents,' Martha called out after her.

In her dreams, Josephat's wife turned to follow the sound of a crying child. At Hartley Mine, her husband Josephat eased himself out of the foreman's wife's friend Rebecca who kept the bottle store. He turned his mind to the increasing joylessness of his marriage bed. Before, his wife had opened all of herself to him, had taken all of him in, rising, rising, rising to meet him, before falling, falling down with him.

Now it was only after prayers for a child that she lay back, her eye only on the outcome. *It is a matter of course that we will have children,* Josephat had thought when they married. *Boys, naturally. Two boys, and maybe a girl.*

He no longer cared what came. All he wanted was to stop the pain. He eased himself out of Rebecca, lay back, and thought of his wife in Easterly.

The winter of the birth of Martha's child was a winter of broken promises. The government promised that prices would go down and salaries up. Instead, the opposite happened. The opposition promised that there would be protests. Instead they bickered over who should hold three of the top six positions of leadership. From the skies fell *chimvuram-abwe,* hailstones of frozen heat that melted on the laughing tongues of Easterly's children. The children jabbed fingers at the corpses of the frogs petrified in the stream near the Farm. The water tap burst.

*Mai*James and *Ba*Toby argued over whether this winter was colder than the one in the last year but one of the war. *Mai*James spoke for the winter of the war, *Ba*Toby for the present winter. 'You were no higher than Toby *uyu,*' *Mai*James said with no rancour. 'What can you possibly remember about that last winter but one?'

It was the government that settled the matter.

'Our satellite images indicate that a warm front is expected from the Eastern Highlands. The warm weather is expected to hold, so pack away those heaters and jerseys. And a very good night to you from your friendly meteorologist, Stan Mukasa. You are listening to *nhepfenyuro yenyu*, Radio Zimbabwe. Over to Nathaniel Moyo now, with *You and Your Farm*.'

This meant that *Ba*Toby was right. If the government said inflation would go down, it was sure to rise. If they said there was a bumper harvest, starvation would follow. 'If the government says the sky is blue, we should all look up to check,' said *Ba*Toby.

That winter brought the threat of more evictions. There had been talk of evictions before, there was nothing new there. They brushed it aside and put more illegal firewood on their fires. Godwills Mabhena who lived next to *Mai*James burnt his best trousers.

———

By the middle of that winter, all of Easterly knew that Martha was expecting a child. The men made ribald comments about where she could have found a man to do the deed. The women worked to convince themselves that it was a matter external to Easterly, to themselves, to their men. 'You know how she disappears for days on end sometimes,' said *Mai*Toby. 'And you know how wild some of those street kids are.'

'Street kids? Some of them are men.'

'My point exactly.'

'Should someone not do something, I don't know, call someone, maybe the police?' asked the female half of the couple whom nobody really knew.

'Yes, you are very right,' said *Mai*James.

28

'Someone should do something.'

'That woman acts like we are in the suburbs,' *Mai*James later said to *Mai*Toby. 'Police? Easterly? *Ho-do!*' They clapped hands together as they laughed.

'*Haiwa*, even if you call them, would they come? It took what, two days for them to come that time when Titus Zunguza . . .'

'*Ndizvo*, they will not come if *we* have a problem, what about for Martha?'

'And even if they did, what then?'

The female half of the couple that no one really knew remembered that her brother's wife attended the same church as a woman who worked in social welfare. 'You mean Maggie,' her brother's wife said. 'Maggie moved *ku*South with her husband long back. I am sure by now her husband drives a really good car, *mbishi chaiyo.*'

She got the number of the social department from the directory. But the number she dialled was out of service, and after three more attempts, she gave it up. *There is time enough to do something*, she thought.

And when the children ran around Martha and laughed, 'Go and play somewhere else,' *Mai*Toby scolded them. 'Did your mothers not teach you to respect your elders? And as for you, *wemazinzeve*,' she turned to Tobias. 'Come and wash yourself.'

The winter of Martha's baby was the winter of Josephat's leave from the mine. It was Easterly's last winter.

On the night that Martha gave birth, Josephat's wife walked to Easterly from a praying field near Mabvuku. She did not notice the residents gathered in clusters around their homes. Only when she walked past Martha's house did the sounds of Easterly reach her. Was that a moan, she wondered. Yes, that sounded like a cry of pain. Without thinking, she walked-ran into Martha's house. By the light of the moon falling through the plastic sheeting, she saw Martha, naked on her mattress, the head of her baby between her legs.

'I'll get help,' Josephat's wife said. 'I'll get help.'

She made for the door. Another moan stopped her and she turned back. She knelt by the mattress and looked between Martha's legs. 'Twenty cents,' Martha said and fainted.

Josephat's wife dug into the still woman and grabbed a shoulder. Her hand slipped.

She cried tears of frustration. Again, she dug, she pulled, she eased the baby out. Martha's blood flowed onto the mattress. 'Tie the cord,' Josephat's wife said out loud and tied it.

She looked around for something with which to cut the cord. There was nothing, and the baby almost slipped from her hands. Through a film of tears she chewed on Martha's flesh, closing her mind to the taste of blood, she chewed and tugged on the cord until the baby was free. She wiped the blood from her mouth with the back of her hand. The baby cried, she held it to her chest, and felt an answering rise in her breasts. She sobbed out laughter. Her heart loud in her chest, she took up the first thing she saw, a poppy-covered dress, and wrapped the baby in it.

In her house she heated water and wiped

the baby clean. She dressed it in the clothes of the children who had slipped from her. She put the baby to breast and he sucked on air until both fell asleep. This was the vision that met Josephat when he returned after midnight. 'Whose child is that?'

'God has given me this child,' she said.

In the half-light Josephat saw his wife's face and his stomach turned to water. 'I will go to the police,' he said. 'You cannot snatch a child and expect me to do nothing.'

His wife clutched the baby closer. 'This is God's will. We cannot let Martha look after it. How can we let her look after a child?'

'What are you talking about, who is Martha?'

'Martha Martha, I left her in her house, she gave birth to it. She can't look after it, this is God's will.'

Josephat blundered out of the room. He knew with certainty that it was just as he thought. Ten months before he had arrived home, and found his wife not there. 'She has gone to an all-night prayer session,' a neighbour said. A wave of anger and repulsion washed over him. He had only this and the next night before he was to go back to the mine.

A wasted journey, he thought.

He had gone to the beer garden in Mabvuku. The smell of his wife was in the blankets when he returned, but she wasn't home. The hunger for a woman came over him. He left his house to urinate and relieved himself against the wall through the pain of his erection. A movement to the right caught his eye. He saw the shape of a woman. His mind turned immediately to thoughts of sorcery. He lit a cigarette and in the flare of the match saw the mad woman. 'May I have twenty cents,' she said, and lifted her up dress.

He had followed the woman to her house in the corner, grappled her to the ground, forced himself on her, let himself go, and in that moment came to himself. 'Forgive me,' he said, 'forgive me.'

He did not look at her until she said, 'May I have twenty cents.' He looked at her smiling face with horror; he fell over his trousers and backwards into the door. He pulled up his trousers as he ran and did not stop running until he reached his house. 'It is not me,' he had said again and again. 'This is not me.'

He lit a cigarette. There was a smell of burning filter. He had lit the wrong end. He bargained with God, he bargained with the spirits on both his mother's and his father's sides. He bargained with himself. He would touch no woman other than his wife. He would not leave her, even if she never bore him a child. And even as he later gave in to Rebecca, to Juliet, and the others, he told himself that these others meant nothing at all.

Josephat found Martha lying on the floor on her back. He raised her left arm, it fell back. He covered her body with a blanket, and left the house. Snatches of conversation reached his ears from the group gathered around *Ba-*Toby. For the first time he realised that Easterly was still awake, unusually so; it was well after midnight and yet here were people gathered around in knots in the moonlight. He moved close, he had to know.

'They were at Union Avenue today, they took all the wares.'

'They just threw everything in the back of the lorries.'

'Didn't care what they broke. Just threw everything.'

'In Mufakose it was the same, they destroyed everything.'

'Siyaso is gone, Mupedzanhamo too.'

'Union Avenue flea market.'

'*Kwese neku*Africa Unity, it is all cleared.'

'Even *kuma*suburbs, they attacked Chisipite market.'

'My cousin-brother said they will come for the houses next.'

'They would not dare.'

'*Hanzi* there are bulldozers at Porta Farm as we speak.'

'If they can destroy Siyaso . . .'

'But they can't destroy Siyaso.'

'That is not possible,' said *Ba*Toby. 'I will not believe it.'

'I was there,' Godwills Mabhena said. 'I was there.'

'You men, the only thing you know is to talk and talk,' *Mai*James said. 'Where are you when action is required? Where were you when they took down Siyaso? *Nyarara-zvako.*' The last word of comfort was directed to the crying child on her hip. His mother was one of three women arrested in Mufakose, two for attempting to take their clothes off in protest, the third, the child's mother, for clinging to her box of produce even as a truncheon came down, again, again, on her bleeding knuckles. The child sniffled into *Mai*James's bosom.

'I will not believe it,' *Ba*Toby said again.

———

In his house Josephat took down a navy-blue suitcase and threw clothes into it. His wife held the baby in a tender lock and crooned a lullaby that Josephat's own mother had sung to him.

'Your child will not be consoled, sister.'

'We are leaving,' he said.

'She cries for her mother, gone away.'

'We have to pack and leave.'

'Gone away, to Chidyamupunga.'

'The bulldozers are coming.'

'Chidyamupunga, cucumbers are rotting.'

'We have to leave now.'

'Cucumbers are rotting beyond Mungezi.'

'Ellen, please.'

She looked up at him. He swallowed. Her smile in the half-light put him in mind

39

of Martha. 'We have to leave,' he said. He picked up an armful of baby clothes. He held them in his hands for a moment, then stuffed them into the suitcase and closed it.

'It is time to go,' he said. As they walked, to Josephat's mind came the words of his mother's lullaby.

Cucumbers are rotting beyond Mungezi.
Beyond Mungezi there is a big white knife,
A big white knife to cut good meat,
To cut good meat dried on a dry bare rock . . .

They stole out of Easterly Farm and into the dawn.

When the morning rose over Easterly, not even the children noticed Martha's absence. They were running away from the bulldozers. It was only when Josephat and his wife had almost reached Chegutu that the bulldozers, having razed the entire line of houses from *Mai*James to *Ba*Toby, having crushed beneath them the house from which Josephat and his wife had fled, and having razed that of the new couple that no one really knew, finally lumbered towards Martha's house in the corner and exposed her body, stiff in death, her child's afterbirth wedged between her legs.